City of the Roborgs

David Orme

Stanley Thornes (Publishers) Ltd

First published in 1996 by:
Stanley Thornes (Publishers) Ltd
Ellenborough House
Wellington Street
CHELTENHAM GL50 1YW
England

A catalogue record for this book is available from the British Library.

ISBN 0 7487 2588 1

Cover artwork by Paul McCaffrey
Typeset by Tech-Set, Gateshead
Printed and bound in Great Britain at Martin's The Printers, Berwick

1

It was Mrs Traven's birthday. She was seventy today. This week she would get a letter from the hospital to tell her that it was time for her Final Sleep. She had lived a busy and useful life. Now it was time for her to die to make room for someone else.

Mrs Traven lived next door to Mina Ransom. Mina was seventeen. She had known Mrs Traven all her life. She would miss her.

'Why does she have to go for the Final Sleep?' she complained to her parents. 'Why can't she live until she dies of old age?'

Her parents looked shocked. 'You know very well, Mina,' they said. 'The old must die to make room for the new. The world can't support people who can't work. Besides, who wants to live until they're too old to look after themselves? The Final Sleep is a beautiful end to a life.'

Mina lived with her parents in a tiny flat on the forty-second level. Every day she went to college. At college she spent each morning on the educator machine. This was linked directly to her brain. She was taught useful skills, and how to be a good citizen. In the afternoon there was sport, and sometimes lectures from important people. Soon she would finish her education and start working. She spent her whole life in the huge city. Most of it was underground. Very few people had ever seen the open country outside the city.

Mina liked Mrs Traven. Only that morning the old lady had called her into her little flat. She was holding a package wrapped up in paper.

'This is a present for you,' she had said. 'Don't open it until I've gone, and don't show it to your parents, and especially not your uncle. It's a secret.'

Mina had done as Mrs Traven had asked. She had hidden the parcel in her bedroom.

When Mina got home from school three days later someone was moving into Mrs Traven's flat. It was a young couple. They seemed nice people, but Mina couldn't help thinking about her old friend, who had gone to her Final Sleep.

After the meal her parent settled down to watch a T.V. show. 'Come and watch, Mina,' they said. 'It's your Uncle Richard.'

Mina's uncle was someone very important in the government. The family were very proud to have such an important relative. He was telling all the viewers that the harvests had been bad, and that rations would have to be reduced. Everyone would have to work harder. This didn't sound very interesting.

'I'm tired,' said Mina. 'I'm going for a lie down.'

As soon as she had shut her bedroom door behind her, she took out Mrs Traven's present. She tore off the paper. It was an old book, with a red cover and pages brown with age.

Mina had heard of books, but she had never seen one. All knowledge came from computers and T.V. She knew that books were forbidden. The book was very fragile. She turned the pages very carefully, and started to read. At first it didn't make any sense, but she carried on. Soon she couldn't put the book down.

2

The next day Mina was due for her regular check-up at the hospital. Everyone went to the hospital once every three months. Many tests were done, and small illnesses could be spotted and cured before they became serious. It was a worrying time. Anyone found to have a serious illness would be sent for the Final Sleep. Sick people were not useful. They had to make way for others.

On the way Mina kept thinking about the old book. It was a book of stories. The stories were about people living their lives many years ago. Mina had learnt that people lived in houses of their own, out in the open air. They could choose where they wanted to live, and who they married. They could even choose what job they wanted to do. No one went for the Final Sleep. Hospitals tried to keep people alive as long as possible.

All this seemed impossible to Mina. Life in the past seemed wonderful compared to life now.

There was a long queue at the hospital. The staff there were always busy and bad-tempered. At last Mina's turn came. She went into a small room. A sample of blood was taken from her arm. They she lay down and a large scanning machine moved across her. A man sitting at a computer screen checked the results.

'Next,' he called out, without looking at Mina.

Mina walked home. Sometimes it was possible to travel on the moving pavements, but these had been closed down to save energy. Now people walked everywhere. They had to get up earlier to get to work. No one grumbled. There were punishments for people who always complained. It was easier just to put up with things.

When Mina got home she had a surprise. Her parents should have been at work, but they were at home sitting in the living-room. They looked frightened and worried. Another person was in the room. It was Uncle Richard. On the table in front of them was the red book.

Mina's father spoke first. 'Where did you get this?'

Mina went red and hung her head. 'Old Mrs Traven gave it to me before she went for her Final Sleep.'

Uncle Richard spoke. 'You know that books are forbidden?'

Mina didn't say anything.

'Answer your uncle, Mina,' said her mother.

Mina nodded her head.

Uncle Richard opened a briefcase and put the book inside.

'You are an intelligent girl, Mina. I've been looking at your report from college. Something like this could spoil your whole future. Have you read any of this?'

Mina was still too frightened to talk. She nodded her head.

Uncle Richard sighed. 'You are lucky, then, that I am your uncle! Thank goodness your parents spoke to me when they found this. Now, Mina, you are nearly ready to leave college. I want you to come with me now. I have a special job for you. Say goodbye to your parents.'

Mina saw to her horror that a bag had already been packed for her. She started to cry. Deep sobs shook her body. Her parents didn't seem to notice. They kissed her once, then sat down and turned on the television. Uncle Richard took hold of her arm. A tall man in a grey suit came in through the front door. He held Mina's other arm. Suddenly Mina knew she was leaving her home forever.

3

Every corridor had lifts that took people from one level to another. The lifts didn't always work, and people had to use the stairs. Uncle Richard and the grey-suited man led Mina to the nearest lift.

Uncle Richard pressed his finger into a small hole in the wall. This read his fingerprint. He tapped some numbers into the keypad. The lift set off downwards.

The floors flashed by. Mina had never been so deep before. Normally people were not allowed in the lower levels, where the food and energy plants were. The lift seemed to be going even deeper than that.

At last the lift stopped. Mina had not asked any questions about where she was going. She was still too shocked and upset.

The lift opened. The corridor looked just like the one outside Mina's home. They walked down it to a moving pavement.

At first the corridors seemed empty. Then she saw a group of figures in the distance coming towards her.

There were four figures on the pavement. When they came close, Mina gasped in horror. Were they people or machines? One side of their heads and faces seemed normal, but the other seemed to be made of shiny plastic. In the plastic a glass lens took the place of an eye.

There was something strange and not human about the arms and legs, too. One of the strange creatures had a claw instead of a hand. They were all bald, and had a sort of metal cage over the tops of their heads. Mina noticed that they all had a number on their shoulders. They all saluted Uncle Richard as they passed.

'What are those things?' said Mina with a shudder. 'They're horrible.'

Uncle Richard smiled. 'Not so horrible when you get used to them, my dear. They're roborgs. People with the strength of robots and the minds of computers. So much better than us ordinary people. You are a very lucky girl, Mina. Not many people have visited the City of the Roborgs!'

Mina found her voice at last. 'But I don't want to be here. I want to go home. You can't keep me here!'

Uncle Richard never stopped smiling. He always smiled, even when he was on the television giving bad news.

'Oh no, Mina. You can't go home. You know why, don't you?'

Mina shook her head.

'Because you are a trouble-maker, Mina. There is no room in the city for trouble-makers. If there is no room for you, you know what will happen.'

Mina felt a terrible coldness inside her. She knew what happened to trouble-makers – the Final Sleep.

4

Even though she was frightened and upset, Mina was still amazed by the underground city. Great open spaces were brightly lit. All the moving pavements were working.

The streets and corridors were full of roborgs. Mina thought she could never get used to the sight of these half-human, half-robot creatures. She looked but could see no human beings except herself, her uncle and the man in grey.

'Are there no other people here?'

Her uncle shook his head. 'Not many now. Once people see what the roborgs can do, they aren't satisfied. They ask to become roborgs. One day I will be a roborg too.'

They changed to another moving pavement. Soon Mina found she was in a vast underground space. Machines hummed and lights winked on and off.

'The life of the city starts here,' said Uncle Richard. 'Over there is the big power plant. It make the city's electricity. Next to it are the great pumps, to pump fresh water to everyone. In the next hall is the great food-making plant. Without all this the city above would die.'

Soon they reached a room with great glass windows. It seemed to be fixed in the roof of the huge underground city.

14

Uncle Richard put his finger into a hole, then gazed into a tiny bright light. The door opened.

'This is the control centre,' he said. 'From here I can control everything that happens in the city. Watch this!'

He spoke into a microphone. 'Roborgs, stop!'

At once, every roborg in sight stood absolutely still. Uncle Richard spoke again. 'Roborgs, carry on!'

Mina thought it was horrible. 'Why would anyone want to be a roborg? They have no minds of their own!'

'Not all of them are like that. Some roborgs keep their human minds.'

'But who were all these people?'

'Can't you guess, Mina? Not everyone who goes for the Final Sleep is old. These are trouble-makers. We recycle their bodies here. A human body is far too valuable to throw away.'

Uncle Richard turned and opened another door. 'Welcome to my home, Mina. It is going to be your home for a short while.'

They all went inside. Mina gasped. It was beautiful!

Shelves were full of fine carvings and pottery. There were rich carpets on the floor. The furniture was very grand. A door was open into another room. Inside that room Mina saw shelves and shelves of books!

Uncle Richard took Mina's red book out of his case.

'Another book for my collection! Now, Mina, I have prepared a room for you. I hope you will be comfortable in it. You will stay in it until your operation can be arranged. Hunter here will look after you.' The man in the grey suit stepped forward.

'What operation?' asked Mina, shocked. 'There's nothing wrong with me!'

'Nothing at all,' agreed Uncle Richard. 'You're perfect in every way, and very intelligent. But soon you'll be even better than you are now.'

'What do you mean?'

'I'm going to turn you into a roborg, Mina.'

5

Mina found herself lying on a soft bed. For a moment she couldn't remember where she was.

Then everything came flooding back. The book, her uncle, the journey to the City of the Roborgs, the terrible thing he had said he would do to her. She could remember that she had screamed and had tried to hit her uncle. She had felt a sharp pain. Hunter, the man in grey, had injected her with something.

She sat up and look around. It was a very beautiful room. She got off the bed and crossed to the door. She was locked in.

Just then the T.V. screen in the wall came to life. Uncle Richard's face looked out at her.

'Now, Mina, it is important for you to know what is going to happen to you. I know it is difficult for you to accept. Trust me. Once you have had the operation you will be much happier than you are now. All those nasty feelings will be gone. You will help to make the wonderful new Earth we are all working for.'

The screen changed. There were scenes from old films from the past of terrible wars, and people starving.

'This is how we once were. Now no one gets angry, and no one starves. Every drop of water people drink has special drugs in it to stop people being upset or aggressive.'

Mina was stunned. The water they all drank – drugged! She remembered how her parents had been so calm about her leaving. All they wanted to do was watch television.

'For most people, the drugs work well. But for some people the drugs stop working as they grow older. People like you, Mina. Your hospital report said so. If we did nothing you would be very unhappy. You would start to cause trouble. But you are too special to be sent for the Final Sleep. We need intelligent people – as roborgs! You must prepare yourself. Your operation is tomorrow!'

Uncle Richard was still smiling. 'Trust me, Mina. Being a roborg is a wonderful thing.'

Mina rushed to the screen. She beat it with her fists and screamed. But the picture was gone.

Mina slept heavily during the night period. When she woke up, she guessed she had been drugged. She had not eaten the food or drunk the water. Perhaps the drug had come through the air supply.

She felt quite calm and relaxed. It was almost as if she was not in control of her body. She knew she had to do what she was told.

Soon the door opened and Hunter came in. 'Come,' he said.

Mina followed him out of the fine rooms. A door behind a curtain led into a corridor. Three roborgs were waiting for her. They surrounded her and led her to the moving pavement. Mina knew she had to obey them. Hunter watched her go. He didn't move or speak.

As they passed a dark opening to another corridor there came a deafening bang, followed by two more. The head of the roborg in front of her exploded in a mess of red flesh and bone and metal parts. Mina turned, and saw the other two roborgs lying on the ground. One had a burning hole in the chest. The other had lost an arm and was making a horrible howling noise.

Four figures carrying large and dangerous-looking weapons rushed out of the dark corridor. One of them stood over the injured roborg and aimed the weapon at its head. There was another bang and the head exploded, splattering the corridor with red.

Mina still felt nothing. It was like a dream.

'She's been drugged,' someone shouted. 'Bring her this way. Drag her if you need to. Quick! The alarm's started!'

A loud wailing sound could be heard along the corridors. The injured roborg had managed to send an alarm before he was killed. Mina felt herself being roughly grabbed. She knew she was running along the dark corridor. She still didn't feel she was really there at all.

6

Mina's head was spinning and her eyes were closed. The alarm still sounded. She could hear the sound of running feet. She was standing still now. Slowly she opened her eyes.

In front of her was a fair-haired young man. He put down his weapon and took a small piece of equipment from his pocket. He pressed it to the wall. At once a wall panel opened. Mina stared. Who was this young man? Who were the other three?

The strangers grabbed Mina and pulled her through the gap. The panel closed behind them.

They were in a passage. It was a kind of passage Mina had never seen before. It was rough and rocky. The floor was uneven.

Mina was feeling better now. Who could these people be? At least they weren't roborgs. She groaned and rubbed her eyes.

'Are you feeling better?' said the young man with fair hair. 'Don't worry, you're safe now.'

'Who are you?' asked Mina. 'Where are you taking me?'

'You'll find out all that soon. Just keep moving. We need to get to the entrance quickly.'

The tunnel was dark but the four rescuers carried torches. Mina saw that there were two men and two women.

After a long and uncomfortable walk, Mina felt a strange, cold wind on her face. The walls of the passage disappeared. There seemed to be a huge space in front of her. Above her, tiny points shone down.

One of the young women in the group came over to Mina. 'My name is Sue. We call ourselves outsiders. I don't suppose you have been in the open before. Don't worry, you're quite safe.'

The open! Mina had seen films of the great fields around the city. Robot tractors ploughed the soil and gathered their crops. Mina knew that the world had many cities like her own. All the rest of the world was covered in fields apart from the highest mountains.

She looked up. 'Are they stars?' she asked. What a wonderful sight!

'Yes, but we can't stop to look now. There might be a roborg patrol out. Quickly, over here.'

The group moved on. It was very dark. Mina couldn't see

where she was going but she could feel trees and bushes brushing against her. She knew what they were. She had seen trees and bushes in the city parks.

'Get in!'

She found herself being pushed into a seat in a large metal box. The others piled in as well. A door slammed. She heard an engine starting, and the whole box started to move!

'It's called a car. There are no moving pavements out here!'

There was very little to see outside the car. It was a very dark night, and a long journey. At one point the car stopped. Mina heard liquid gurgling, and she guessed that someone was putting fuel in the car.

One the way the four young people explained a little. It all seemed confusing to Mina.

'We live outside the city. There are hundreds of us. Sometimes we break into the city. We steal things and try to cause trouble. We saw you and guessed what was going to happen to you, so we rescued you.'

'But why do you want to cause trouble?'

'We'll explain that all later, when we get back home.'

The night wasn't as dark now. Mina could see things outside the car.

'Nearly morning,' said Sue. 'Luckily we're nearly there.'

At last the car stopped in a rocky valley.

'Come indoors, quickly,' said Sue. 'If you haven't been in the open before, it can be frightening.'

A door opened and Mina was taken into a small room. An old man with white hair was cooking a meal in a corner. He came over. 'Welcome!' he said. 'Welcome to freedom!'

7

The food was strange but tasted good.

'It's real food, Mina,' said the old man. 'And there are no drugs in it!'

The room seemed full when everybody crowded in. There were only a few chairs and most people sat on the floor.

Mina remembered the question she had asked on the way. 'Why do you want to cause trouble in the city? Trouble-makers are bad people.'

The old man smiled. 'Not all trouble-makers, Mina! Besides, we only want to damage the City of the Roborgs. One day, we will destroy it, and all the poor, drugged people from the upper levels can come out into the sunshine.'

'But there isn't room! The planet is crowded with cities. All of the land is used for food. People have to stay in the cities.'

The old man smiled. 'Finish your food and come with me, Mina.'

Outside it was not quite light. The old man and his friends led her out of the little room. It had wheels on it. They told Mina it was called a caravan.

At first, Mina was frightened by the huge spaces outside. She had never seen a real sky. When she looked up she felt suddenly dizzy.

They set off up a climbing path. It ran through trees. Mina was pleased as it hid the frightening sky. The path got steeper and steeper but the old man didn't slow down. At last they came to a rocky open place.

Mina gasped and almost fell. Sue held her tightly. They were on the top of a high hill. They could see for miles. There were forests, and high hills in the distance. In the valley below a wide river glittered in the sun.

Mina found herself sobbing. She had never seen anything so beautiful in her life.

Back in the caravan the old man, whose name was Daniel, explained things to Mina. 'The world isn't full of cities. That's a lie! There is only one city, with fields around it. The rest of the world is wild and empty. It is a beautiful world! Once there was a terrible war. Nearly everyone died. The few people that lived built a city under the ground to protect them from the terrible radiation. The radiation has gone, but still everyone is forced to live in the city, apart from a few who have escaped.'

'But why are they forced to live there?'

'For hundreds of years the city has been controlled by one family. At first, they were good rulers. Later, they started to control people with drugs. Now they have roborgs. Without the city they would lose all their power. We think the present ruler plans to destroy all human beings except himself. Richard Ransom is a madman!'

Mina gasped when she heard the name. 'Ransom is *my* name. He is my uncle!'

8

There was a sudden silence in the caravan. Then a big man called Tony came over to her. 'Richard Ransom's niece!' he said. 'A spy! We'll send her back to him in pieces!'

Daniel stepped between them. 'Don't jump to conclusions, Tony. So you are Mina Ransom? Tell us your story, quickly!'

As quickly as she could, Mina told her story. The book, the hospital visit, the journey to the City of the Roborgs, the threat her uncle had made to her. Daniel looked her in the face.

'I believe her!' he said. 'Tony, sit down, you fool. Mina, are you with us? Will you help us destroy your uncle, and the city?'

Mina nodded. 'I don't know what I can do, but I will help. I would rather die than be a roborg.'

Daniel and his group spent many days making plans and preparations. At night they all slept in tents around the caravan. They moved camp several times in case the roborgs had located them. The caravan was fixed behind the car and was towed slowly along rutted roads at night. The word had spread and many other groups came to join them.

At last Daniel called Mina into the caravan. 'We are going back to the city tomorrow night,' he said. 'You will guide us to the control centre and your uncle's home. The guards will see you and call your uncle. We will be ready for him.'

He looked serious. 'It's very dangerous. You must take a big risk, Mina.'

Mina nodded. 'I understand. But what will you do when you capture my uncle?'

Daniel showed her a small silver disk. 'We will force him to open the control centre door. Then I will broadcast this over the roborg control system you told us about. It is Ransom's voice ordering the roborgs to kill themselves!'

'But how?'

I have used a computer to create his voice, using old T.V. broadcasts. We're not primitive just because we live in the open air, you know!'

The next night a fleet of cars and even horse-drawn carts set off for the city. Mina had a new experience that evening – rain. She couldn't help thinking what a waste of water it was!

Soon a band of two or three hundred well-armed outsiders were creeping along the secret passage. Tony was in the lead. He kept looking at Mina with a frown on his face. She knew he still didn't trust her.

At last they reached the city wall and Tony opened the panel. The people with weapons climbed through. Daniel stayed close to Mina. He was their leader, but was too old for fighting.

'Remember, when you see a roborg, you must go for the head,' said Tony. 'They are very strong. If you just injure them, they will be able to send a message. It must be a clean kill.'

Soon they reached a main passage. Mina stopped. She had been drugged when she came from her uncle's room, and it was difficult to remember which was the right way.

'Down here,' she said at last.

They set off down the wide corridor. They turned a corner and Mina realised that they weren't in the corridor leading to her uncle's room. They were in the great open space of the city!

The space was full of roborgs. They turned to look at the outsiders. At once an alarm sounded through the city.

Tony glared at Mina. 'You led us into this trap. I knew you were a spy and a traitor!' he said. He raised his weapon and pointed it at her. 'But you'll be the first to die!'

9

Mina was frozen to the spot. She stared at the big gun. It was pointing to her head. She remembered the roborgs and how their heads had exploded.

There was a sharp bang and the weapon seemed to leap out of Tony's hands. He cried out in pain and clutched his injured hand.

'Quick, back into the passage!' This came from Sue. She was second in command.

Most of the outsiders were still in the passage. Sue and the other leaders ran quickly back. Mina ran with them.

'Aren't you going to stay with your friends now?' sneered Sue.

'They're not my friends. I'm on your side. I just lost my way.'

The young fighters did not believe her. Even Daniel looked stunned at what had happened.

'Finish her off now, I say,' said Tony. Blood was dripping from his injured hand.

'No,' said Sue. 'She's coming back with us. She's far too useful to kill. Back to the tunnel!'

Suddenly they heard the tramp of roborg feet. It came from behind them.

'Trapped!' groaned Tony. 'We're finished!'

Roborgs were coming at them from both sides. The outsiders set up their heavy weapons and fired. Many of the roborgs were injured or killed, but still they came. Soon the passage behind was almost blocked with shattered and bleeding roborgs.

'Why aren't they firing?' shouted Sue, as she loaded her weapon once more.

Tony pointed to Mina. 'That's why. They want our little roborg-lover alive!'

Just then there was a hiss of gas. White clouds spread along the corridor. Mina felt herself falling. The world went dark . . .

Slowly Mina opened her eyes. She felt stiff and sore. She found herself back in the room in her uncle's house. There must have been a camera watching her. She heard her uncle's voice.

'Well, Mina, now your adventure is over. I'm coming in to see you. Prepare yourself, for I have changed.'

The door opened. In stepped – a roborg! And yet half of its face was that of Uncle Richard!

'Yes, Mina, I'm a roborg now. Soon, you will be one too. Listen to me, Mina! Even roborgs cannot live forever. I am old now. When I die, you will be the new ruler of the city! You are strong and intelligent. You will carry on our family's great experiment! First I need to make you more obedient. You will learn this now, Mina. Hunter! Bring the drug!'

Hunter, still wearing his grey suit, came into the room. He carried a needle. Mina knew she was about to be injected with a terrible drug. 'No! I won't!'

She jumped from the bed, but her uncle was ready for her. His powerful roborg arms held her down. Hunter came across to the bed. She saw the evil needle. Hunter bent over and stabbed the needle firmly into . . . Uncle Richard!

For one second his eyes looked shocked. Then they seemed to go dull. He crashed to the floor.

10

Hunter felt Uncle Richard's neck. 'He's dead, miss.'

'But why did you do it? Was it to save me?'

Hunter nodded. 'Partly, miss. You see, he was going to make me a roborg too. I pretended I wanted it to happen. But I didn't. I wanted to get away. I've been waiting for this chance.'

'What are we going to do now?'

'It's up to you, miss. You're our leader now.'

'What about my friends, the outsiders? Where are they now?'

'They're all safe, miss. The roborgs have them locked up. They were lined up to become roborgs, too.'

Mina went out into the big room. Opposite was the door into the control centre. She pulled at the door but it would not open. Then she remembered how her uncle opened doors. He put his finger in a hole. Then he gazed into the bright light. These recognised his fingerprint and the pattern in his eye.

'How are we going to open the door?' An awful thought struck her. 'Do we have to . . . '

Hunter shook his head. 'We don't have to cut his finger off or dig his eye out! You're the leader now. It will work for you.'

Mina put her finger in the hole and peered into the light. The door opened.

'Go on, miss. Use the microphone. You're in charge now!'

Mina spoke. She felt very nervous. 'Roborgs! Bring the leaders of the outsiders to the control centre!'

Soon Sue, Tony and Daniel were standing before her. They looked angry and bitter.

'What are you going to do to us?' asked Tony. 'I will never be a roborg! I will kill myself first! Where is you uncle?'

'My uncle is dead. You were wrong, I was never on his side.'

They looked at Mina, then at each other.

'It's just a trick,' said Tony.

Daniel took the small silver disk from his pocket.

'I think you're telling the truth,' he said. 'Prove it by playing this! It is your uncle's voice. It tells the roborgs to destroy themselves. Play it now!'

'They won't listen,' said Mina. 'They know my uncle is dead so they will not obey his voice. I am the leader. They will do what I say. But I am not going to kill the roborgs.'

Tony took two steps forward. His face was angry.

'We will need them to destroy the drugs that control the city above. After that, I still won't have them killed. Once they were people. Good people. Uncle called them trouble-makers. The world outside is going to need people like that. Maybe we can change them back into people again. At least I am going to try.'

Tony relaxed. At last he knew she was telling the truth.

Daniel looked at Mina. 'Now you are the new leader. You have great power! What are you going to do with it?'

Mina shook her head. 'My family has caused enough harm! I will not be a leader. Once an old lady gave me a book. It was about the world before the terrible war. People chose their leaders then. They weren't told how to live their lives. They could live until they were old. If we all work together, we can make the world like that again.'

She turned and spoke into the microphone. Outside, the roborgs listened to their new orders. The people of the city were about to start a new life.